A Touch of Sepia

By Anne-Maree Althaus

Of all the people who live in our street, Mrs. Donnelly is my favorite. She's like an extra grandmother to us. Matthew, Laura, and I call her Mrs. D.

She's lived here for over thirty years, watching the buildings grow taller and the city spread wider. She says her little house is a reminder of the past.

The backyard is overgrown and full of leafy hiding places. My favorite time of the year is spring, when the huge jacaranda tree carpets the ground with a layer of purple.

Inside, the rooms are crammed with all sorts of interesting things. It's a perfect place for exploring.

Mrs. D always has a story to tell. It surprises me that she can remember so many details from so long ago, yet she still forgets where she leaves her glasses!

We like listening to her talk about
the games she used to play.
Hopscotch was her favorite, because
she was the champion of her
neighborhood.

Another time, she showed us how to make little tractors from old wooden spools, rubber bands, wooden pegs, and toothpicks. She said her son used to make them. He would construct obstacle courses for the tractors to conquer, and hills for them to climb.

One night, we were staying with Mrs. D while Mom and Dad went to a meeting. It was too dark to go outside and no one felt like watching TV.

I was standing beside the old gramophone, near the window. I stared up at the shelf on the wall and noticed a large, gilt-edged book with a lock on one side.

Mrs. D saw me looking at it and said, "I'll bet your family album doesn't look like that one. Would you like to see it?"

Matthew and Laura ran to get the best seats on the couch. As Mrs. D carefully opened the lock on the book, I felt as though we were about to take a trip back in time.

There were photos of family
members . . .
and picnic scenes . . .
country roads . . .
and city streets.

Laura giggled when she saw the bathing suits . . . and Matthew loved the photograph of the Model-T Ford.

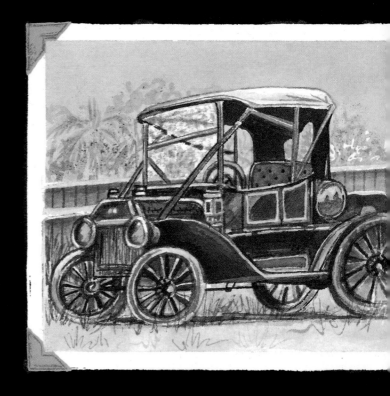

The portrait of Mrs. D and her husband fascinated me. She looked so young. Mrs. D smiled. "Ah, it seems so long ago," she said.

"Hey, there's a picture of your gramophone!" Matthew said, pointing to the next page.

"We used to dance to that," said Mrs. D.

"Does it still work?" asked Laura.

Before long, the sounds of old-time dance music filled the room. Matthew, who loved being a show-off, bowed to Mrs. D and offered his hand. "May I have the pleasure of this dance?" he said.

"I would be delighted, young man," replied Mrs. D.

They couldn't keep in time very well, because Matthew is a pretty hopeless dancer, and they kept bumping into furniture. Laura and I pretended to be the band.

Still, when the music finished, Mrs. D said it was the best dance she'd ever had.

The doorbell rang to tell us that Mom and Dad were back. We said good-bye and, as we walked down the street, I watched the lights in Mrs. D's house go off, one by one.

I wonder what I'll remember when I'm as old as Mrs. D.